THE GIANT THAT SNEEZED

By Norman Leach

Illustrated by Toni Goffe

Child's Play (International) Ltd

Swindon   Sydney   Toronto   New York

© M. Twinn 1993   ISBN 0-85953-927-X   Printed in Singapore

Once there was a very timid Giant.
He was so scared, he wouldn't say Boo to a goose.
Whenever he was frightened,
which was very often indeed, he sneezed.

Giants need a lot more food than the rest of us,
and, usually, they get whatever they ask for.
But this giant was too frightened to ask.
He lived on turnip soup, which he didn't even like.

One day, there were no turnips left,
so he went to find something else to eat.

He walked and walked, until he came to a patch of wild land,
where he found a bean plant with a few beans on it.
He picked the beans on the top and ate them.

He liked the taste of beans much better than turnips,
so he picked the beans in the middle and ate them.
He was still hungry, so he picked the beans at the bottom
and ate them, too.

Now, this bean plant was growing up through a big hole.
So, the Giant climbed very carefully into the hole,
eating beans as he went.

To his surprise, he wasn't underground but up in the air.
The plant was growing up through the clouds from a land
of green fields and pretty little houses far below.

When he looked down, the Giant felt giddy.
"Ooooooh, I'm scared. **A-a-a-tishoo!**"

And he toppled down to the bottom of the plant.

There he was, sitting in a vegetable garden,
next to a farmhouse.

He picked himself up and tapped gently
on the farmhouse door with one finger.

"What do you want?" called a voice from inside.

"A drink of water, if you don't mind," said the Giant.
All those beans had made him thirsty.

A little woman opened the door.

"Oh, my haystacks . . . A giant!
I'll get you some water. But as soon as you've finished,
you had better run away, before my son Jack gets home.
He thinks he's a giant-slayer and he might do something silly."

She brought a bucket of water and the Giant drained it
in one gulp. He was about to ask for another,
when they heard the sound of someone singing.

"Fee, fie, foe, fum.
I smell the smell of a giant's tum.
Be his name Henry or Ivan or Fritz
I'll chop him up into little bits."

"It's Jack," called the little woman. "Run for it!"

The Giant tried, but his legs were rooted to the spot.

"Hide then," cried the little woman.

But the Giant was too big for the hen-house,
too big for the stable and too big for the farm-house.

"Quick! Behind the oak tree," called the little woman.

And that is where he was, when Jack arrived,
slicing the heads off dandelions with his big axe.

The Giant pinched his nose tight
to stop himself sneezing.

"I've been killing giants," said Jack.
"What's for supper, Mother?"

Actually, Jack had been chopping down trees.
But he pretended to himself that they were giants.

"Stop being silly, Jack," said the little woman.
"Come and tell me what you've been doing all day."

Jack's father had gone away, but Jack remembered the stories
he used to tell about Grandpa Jack, the great giant-killer.
Jack believed his father was a hero and that he had gone
to fight giants, too. His mother never spoke about it.

When he had finished supper,
Jack sat in his rocking-chair and started to snooze.

Jack's mother beckoned to the Giant and said,
"It's safe to go now. He's asleep.
Come and see me again. I'll cook you some baked beans."

Just then Jack woke up.

"Who are you talking to, Mother?" he asked.

"Only the dog, Son," she replied. "Go back to sleep."

As Jack dozed off again, the Giant tip-toed
toward the beanstalk. But, just as he reached it,
Jack woke up with a start.

"We haven't got a dog!" he cried.

Then he saw the Giant.

"Wow!" he shouted, grabbing his axe.
"What a whopper!   Frighten my mother, would you?
I'm going to chop you up into little pieces."

Jack really was a brave, if foolish, boy.

"Mercy," cried the Giant.
"Please, spare me.
I was hungry and thirsty
and your kind Mother gave me
a bucket of water and I am sorry.
Please, let me go.
I will never come back, I promise."

"Let you go? Let you go? Impossible!!" shouted Jack.
"Grandpa Jack wouldn't have let you go.
My Dad wouldn't have let you go.
And I won't let you go.

"My family has killed
hundreds of Giants
and good riddance to all of them.
Now, it's my turn."

"Don't be silly, Jack," said his mother.
"You've never even seen a giant before.
And neither did your father. Except once."

"Mother, you are too soft-hearted," said Jack.
"Giants have to be got rid of. They are not like us.
They are big and fierce and they trample on crops and
knock down houses and steal and tell lies and eat children."

"Eat children?" gasped the Giant. "My folks wouldn't eat
children. I wouldn't hurt a fly. I live on turnip soup."

"Then what are you doing here? We don't have any turnips."

"I ran out of turnips and was looking for something else
to eat," explained the Giant. "Then I found the bean plant."

"Aha! So you've been stealing our beans?" said Jack.
"That settles it."

"I didn't know they were your beans. I won't do it again."

"For the sake of my mother, the farm, the bean plant and
for your own good, I have to kill you. It is my duty.
I have no choice."

Jack advanced on the Giant with the axe held high.

"Keep away from me with that thing," sobbed the Giant.
It might go off!"

His words ended in a wet sneeze which blew the axe
out of Jack's hand.

"Sorry," said the Giant, picking up the axe.
He wiped it on his sleeve before handing it back.
"It's all right. It isn't damaged."

"Good," said Jack. "Because now, you are really for it. Stop blubbering and blow your nose."

He raised the axe once more.

When the Giant blew his nose, the noise was deafening . . . Jack dropped the axe.

"Sorry," apologized the Giant.
"Do you ever have days when nothing goes right?"

"Why don't you put your foot on it?" giggled Jack's mother.
"Or on him, for that matter? He could do with a lesson."

This wasn't a very motherly thing to say,
but mothers always know what is best for their children.

The Giant put his giant-sized boot on the axe.

"Stop giggling, Mother," said Jack crossly.
"It isn't funny. And you, Giant, are standing on my axe."

"Oh, dear. I am so confused," said the Giant,
handing back the axe. "Can't we be friends?"

"No, we can't! Now, take your medicine."

Jack raised the axe again.

"A-a-a-tishoo!"

This time, the Giant's sneeze blew the roof
right off the farmhouse and Jack into the duckpond.

The Giant was so busy putting the roof back on,
he didn't hear Jack's calls for help.

"I wonder where Jack is?" he wondered.

"He's behind you!" shouted Jack's mother.

"Oh, no, he isn't," said the Giant,
mistaking the slime-covered figure for a large frog.

"Oh, yes, he is!" repeated Jack's mother. "Do look out!"

"Oh, no, he isn't," said the Giant,
standing back to admire his work and knocking over Jack,
who was just about to raise his axe.

"Oh, yes, I am!" moaned Jack. "You clumsy oaf!
Why don't you turn your head when you sneeze?
Didn't they teach you any manners?"

"Oh, yes, you are!" said the Giant, picking Jack up,
drying him off, and handing him the axe again.
"Please, let's be friends."

"I've told you already. It's my duty
and a matter of family honour," said Jack.

The third time Jack lifted the axe, the third time the Giant sneezed. He blew the roof off the farm, the hen house and the stables. Jack was nowhere to be seen.

"This Giant isn't such a bad chap, after all," mused Jack, as he trudged home. "And Mother seems to like him."

But duty was duty. So, he repeated some words his father had taught him, over and over again: 'Find giants, kill them'.

By the time he got back, the Giant had repaired all the roofs.

"Shouldn't you offer your victim a last request?" said Jack's mother.

"I suppose so," said Jack, who wanted to do things right. "What would you like?"

"I can't think of anything, thank you," replied the Giant.

"How about a nice bowl of bean soup?" suggested Jack's mother.

"That would be nice."

While Jack's mother made some hot bean soup, Jack paced impatiently up and down, repeating to himself over and over, "Find giants. Kill them."

"Take your time," said Jack's mother. But the Giant picked up the cauldron of hot steaming soup and swallowed it down.

As Jack raised his axe for the very last time,
the Giant squeezed his eyes tight shut and held his breath.

"A-a-a-tishoo!"

There has never been such a sneeze.

Jack's mother had laced the soup with pepper.

Jack flew through the air, four times round the world,
before landing in the top branches of a huge tree.

In the tree was a house.
In the house was Jack's father.

"Little Jack, is it really you? Where did you come from?"

"A giant sneezed me here." Jack replied. "How about you?"

"Same thing. Did your mother give him some soup?"

"Yes," said Jack. "How did you know?"

"Just a wild guess. But, tell me,
why were you standing so close to the Giant?"

"I was trying to kill him, Father,
like you taught me. 'Find giants, kill them.' Remember?"

"Stupid boy. I said, 'Kind giants, fill them.'"

"But what about Grandpa Jack's stories?"

"Maybe, in those days, some giants were bad.
But, if you ask me, they got a bad name, because
they were different and we were afraid of them.

Ever since the Giant blew me here, I've been looked after
by a Giantess. You learn a lot living in a tree.
Giants are very kind. Being so big makes them gentle."

Meanwhile, the Giant and Jack's mother had climbed
up the beanstalk and peered through every gap in the clouds
until they found the tree with Jack and his father and
the Giantess.

And they all became friends and lived happily ever after.

THE END